HEARTSONG

ESSAYS ON LOVE AND REDEMPTION

J.A. DIVINE

COPYRIGHT

To my dearest R.,
You are my divine.
Together, we can be:
J.A. Divine
All my love, always.

Table of Contents

1

———————————

THE WRITER

"I am so close; I may look distant.
So completely mixed with you, I may look separate.
So out in the open, I appear hidden.
So silent, because I am constantly talking with you."
Rumi

Her first love was writing. He was her
second love, her Twin Flame. With
her, love and writing survived
hand-in-hand, whereas one would
simply die without the other.

She spoke to him constantly and wrote
to him for years. She never stopped
writing to him, and though he may

not have always acknowledged her words, he treasured each and every keystroke. He was the willing recipient of her every syllable but never told her this.

Her writing kept her away from him and pulled her toward him at the same time.

At first, she only wrote her pain. Then, she wrote her healing. After, her accomplishments, hopes and dreams. The words always flowed. Her mind was rarely silent. She spoke to him without ever uttering a word.

He read with eagerness, everything, always, though he would rarely utter a word to her.

In her own right, she was a published author of her life story. In reality, only he knew her true life story. A story for his eyes only.

In his mind there were always
questions.
"What goes through your mind when
you're writing?" was one.

"Thoughts go through my mind. They
just come. Then the thoughts
become words and the words
become my stories. The words just
come out. My fingers dance on the
keyboard until I have pages filled
with....me."

"Why me? Out of any recipient in the
world, why me?"

"I don't have an answer as to why you.
Maybe it had to be you. Maybe you
were the only one ready to hear
what I had to say."

"How did you know I was ready?"

"The only answer I have is, because
you were. Right now, I'd say that
you know me better than I know

*myself, because I'm more myself in
my words and you've read every
word I've written."*

*"Does that mean when you write I am
on your mind?"*

*"My writing is me, but without you I
wouldn't have my writing."*

*This is a conversation they never had,
a conversation that never took
place. But, one night when she
wanted to say something, her
thoughts became words.*

Her words became her Heartsong.

2
———

WAITING

"She was waiting for him.....
the next knock on her door to be him.
The next text message to be him.
She always wanted it to be him."
N.R. Hart

She waited. It was minutes, then hours.
Then the clock stopped.

Her hair slowly began to flatten. Her
makeup began to dull. Her dress
with a million sparkles started to

*wrinkle. Her shining smile
dimmed.*

*She was alone with the remnants of an
hours-long birthday dinner
scattered about the table.*

*She wondered, to the deepest of his
core, what did he fear, and why did
he fear her most of all.*

*Outwardly, she was a roaring lioness.
Inside, a lamb just wanting to be
held.*

*She captivated him with her writing
and made him run from her
emotions. He feared her roar and
yet yearned for her tenderness. So,
he abandoned her, left her waiting.*

*She was alone, sitting on that chair,
thinking of him.*

*He was her redemption, the one who
could bring her to her knees, the*

*secret that only she knew and held
close to her heart. They were so
alike, yet only she knew about
falling.*

*She knew how to fall and just lay there
or get up and brush herself off.*

*He was afraid to fall, not knowing
what the ground would be like
beside her. It terrified him.*

3

———————————

DESTRUCTION

"Tere dil mein meri saanson ko panaah mil jaye…
there ishq mein mere jann fanaa ho jaye"
Urdu language poem, author unknown
Translation: If my breath found a place in your heart,
I can get destroyed in your love.

When we think of destruction, we think
of loss and devastation. We think of
every negative connotation there
is, overlooking what could be,
blessings in the midst of embers.

In ancient Greek folklore, the Phoenix

*rose from the ashes symbolizing
rebirth, hope, and renewal.*

In the 1983 television mini-series The
Thorn Birds, *based on the book by
Colleen McCullough, a ranch
succumbed to a completely
devastating fire. Despite the
unimaginable loss, including that
of her father and brother, Meggie,
the protagonist, finds a perfectly
intact perfumed rose, which
survived. She presents the rose to
her beloved Ralph, who happens to
be a priest and her forbidden love.*

*At times the Twin Flame connection
can be seen as forbidden and full
of secrets, most of all the secrets
we hide from our own
selves: Uncertainty, doubt, self-
hate, loneliness. All which we hide
in the deepest depths of ourselves.
The Twin Flame protagonist, aka
the runner, is guilty of all these
sins. The antagonist, the chaser,*

*only wants the runner to see the
beauty that is and always has been
inside them.*

Even the title of the movie The Thorn
Birds *is symbolic: "When it finds
the perfect thorn tree, the thorn
bird impales itself on a thorn and
sings the most beautiful song ever
heard as it dies. ... Then, singing
among the savage branches, it
impales itself upon the longest,
sharpest spine. And, dying, it rises
above its own agony to out-carol
the lark and the nightingale." -
Quote from* The Thorn Birds

*Even in death, there is love. Even in
destruction there is love. Love is
only far away if you push it away.
If you accept and surrender, it is
there in a heartbeat.*

I watched The Thorn Birds *when I was
very young. It captivated me,
especially the forbidden love*

*aspect. I wanted that love for
myself, and then you came into my
life.*

*I can get destroyed in your love, and I
want to destroy you with my love
for you. I want to tear down all
your barriers and fears until you
are left naked in front of my eyes.*

*Then, I will clothe you with an armor
of: Forgiveness, compassion,
acceptance and adoration.*

To me, you look perfect always.

*Destroy me in your love, and I will rise
again and stand before you,
holding out my loving arms,
yearning for your embrace.*

4

HOME

"Home is the starting place of love, hope, and dreams."
Author Unknown

You feel like home to me.

Whenever I enter my home, I feel a
comforting breeze like an embrace,
and I imagine you welcoming me
in. I especially love coming home
at twilight when the light on the
mirrors becomes a fading

illumination into another
dimension, night.

No matter the shade of light, in every
mirror where my own inner beauty
is reflected, I see your face. If I am
a light, a beacon, in my reflection,
you and only you are the reason for
my shine.

Sometimes I wish I could break down
the glass, if only I would truly see
you on the other side. You put up
walls and I have to fight a tireless
fight over and over again to break
through. You don't know that, when
I met you, I met myself, and you
became the twilight reflection in
my mirror, purposely obscure yet
always there.

I will never give up tearing through
your walls and crashing through
the mirror which is us.

You fear me, your face in my mirror.

 J.A. DIVINE

*You don't want to see that I am
your exact image. You hide from
me showing you that we are, in
fact, the same.*

*Like you, I was once the poor athlete. I
wasn't the popular one in school. I
was never the attractive one. I
strove to belong in a world where
everyone but me seemed to fit in.*

*Yet, somewhere along the line I came
into my own, and you remained
behind in that long ago world.*

*I would have always picked you first
on my team, and we would laugh at
the fact that we both couldn't hit or
kick a ball to save our lives. We
would make up our own team.*

*You and I together would be popular to
each other. People would gravitate
towards us, drawn to the special
connection we had. To me, you
look like Adonis and Clark Gable*

*combined. In a crowded room, you
would be the one to mesmerize me.*

If you only knew……

I was once like you. I was once afraid.

*I used to be afraid of snakes, until I
held a Ball Python for the first
time. Unlike the slimy and cold
stereotype which snakes have, I
found its skin to be pleasingly
smooth, its body warm. Holding
the snake was actually a very
serene experience.*

*As snakes shed their skin this
symbolizes rebirth, transformation,
immortality, and healing.*

*My writing comes from you, from your
energy that engulfs my heart.
Without you I would just be staring
at a blank sheet of paper.*

As I lay in bed each night, in my home,

*I think of you. I feel your heart
inside mine, and I'm no
longer looking for a heart with
whom to beat now, because you are
there.*

You are home.

5
———

THE KISS

"...Then he touched his lips to hers. Just a touch. But it lit a spark. Then a fire, a sweeping, a diving. She clung to his shoulders and parted her lips and was lost. Utterly, beautifully lost..."
— Roseanna M. White, The Lost Heiress

Just as you are afraid of falling, I'm afraid of what will happen when we fall together.

How can I imagine what breathing in eternity feels like with the divine union of our lips coming as one?

*Your irregular heartbeat combined
with my heart bursting out of my
chest.*

*Shallow breathing, or no breath at all.
In my rapture I will be lost in you.*

You are my heart and soul's protector.

*Your kiss will encompass my every
warm memory from inception:
Following my grandfather in his
garden as he tended to his
vegetables like children. Holidays
at my aunt's house where decadent
dishes abound. The s till inky smell
of a typewriter over forty years
after I first sat at it. The sweetness
of life, the life you breathe into me.*

*If my mouth were a vast ocean, I would
beckon you to dive in and retrieve
the clam which holds a pearl, the
pearl of my soul.*

And I shall inhale your doubt,

J.A. DIVINE

*uncertainty, self-loathing and
replace it with acceptance,
compassion, humility and trust.*

*I imagine your kiss to feel like sunrise,
the sun breaking through into a
new day. The newness of your kiss
breaking light into me and opening
up new possibilities.*

*When I was a child and visited the
dentist, at the end of my visit I got
to pick a prize from the treasure
chest for being a good patient. I
dug through that chest so deeply
until I found the perfect trinket
prize to behold my child eyes.*

*I am still that child, forever seeking a
hidden treasure. Oh, how I wish
you were brave enough to seek
with me. We could go on
adventures together and find life's
prizes to share.*

In your kiss, you capture my soul, and

conjoin it with yours where it belongs.

I could listen to a song on replay one hundred times and still not memorize the entire lyrics. Each time I hear the song my ears pick up a different tone, and the verses take on an entire new meaning. Listening to a song for the hundredth time is just as new as the first where your ears perk up and you must immediately know what song that is, just as I must immediately know what your kiss is like.

I want to dance with you, but I don't know how to dance. I know that the first step is melodious music, and the harmony coming from our hearts. Position of hands doesn't matter as long as I'm in close proximity to you. The only steps I care about learning are the ones which will bring me to your tall

stature and the nearness of you and
your lips.

Let's take the first step together.

Kiss me, hard and passionately. Dance
    with me. Throw me into the raging
    ocean and retrieve me from the
    crashing waves into your arms,
    where I have always belonged.

6

———

LIES

"I lie to myself all the time. But I never believe me."
— S.E. Hinton, The Outsiders

He told her sweet little lies to try and
push her away. He was a true
runner to the core.

She entertained his lies and went along
with him, yet only she knew the
truth which crept to the surface like
a Lotus flower.

"To blossom, the lotus flower must

grow through mud and dirty pond
water. But it blooms anyway.
Though conditions are tough, the
lotus heeds the call of the sun each
morning, breaks the surface of the
water and blooms untouched by the
mud; each petal remains clean and
pure."

He invented a love, a soulmate named
"Liv." Every time his feelings for
his true one was in danger of
surfacing, he brought up "Liv's"
name. He told tales of things they
did together, adventures they had
taken, moments they shared. He
insisted that he and "Liv" were
meant to be together,

He lied behind an imaginary love. This
was his way of pushing her, his
true love, away.

She saw through him as one would see
through a ghost; the façade was
misty yet the beyond was clear.

     J.A. DIVINE

*He slipped up once, a big slip. Once
she was to have gone to his place
of employment. He knew of her
imminent arrival and bolted. He
later wanted to text her an apology
for missing her that day. Instead,
he texted "I'm sorry I needed
you." Quite an interesting
Freudian slip.*

*He missed her that day as well as
needed her. He missed her always.*

*She missed and needed him too, sweet
lies and all.*

*What he didn't know was what she
knew about his "Liv" fantasy for
every time he had feelings for her,
he brought up "Liv" in
conversation. He thought he had
developed a clever ruse, but she
saw through his tales as one would
see through a faint misty fog.*

He saw her as untouchable. He

brought up "Liv" to keep her at arm's length and away from what he truly felt. Ironically, he was in the death profession. "Liv" was a guise for what he truly desired....to "live" in her.

He was afraid to admit that he was scared. He was scared of his own insecurities and whatever fantasies he was trying to uphold. He told stories to himself to hide about what would happen if he was ever honest with himself and said no more lies.

She told him her each and every deep and dark secret. She never lied.

She wanted to shout, "What if everything around you was broken down? What would be left?"

She would.

She would be left standing among his

*broken pieces, gently kneeling, and
putting each and every one back
together again until he was a
standing man whom she could
wrap her arms around, and never
let go.*

$$\frac{7}{}$$

LOVE

"Loving you just goes on
On and on, on and on
And on"
Song It's You by Simply Red

She wanted to be the keeper of his
heart. His protector and the slayer
of all which might threaten his
existence. Gender roles were
thrown to the wayside. She didn't
need him, a man, to be her keeper.
She desired to be his and to keep
his heart safe.

*They both shared the same Chinese
zodiac animal – the tiger. Same
beast with vast individualistic
traits. She was brave and confident
while he was charming and well-
liked. Yet, their souls were the
same.*

*There was once a story of a wounded
Siberian tiger on the China-Russia
border who was injured and came
out of the wild seeking human help.
This behavior is atypical of
Siberian tigers to come out of the
wild. In the end, the tiger got the
help he needed and was healed.*

What she wished she could tell him:

*"You are a wounded Siberian tiger in
the wild, afraid to come out and
seek help, from me least of all.*

*"Should I find you in the wild I would
lie down next to you. I may be
helpless or incapable of healing*

*your wounds, but I would lean my
body against yours so that you
could feel the warmth of my
beating heart. You may fight me.
You may try to push me away, but
my loving hold will only become
stronger.*

*"Should you succumb to your wounds,
I would never leave your side. I
would remain steadfast in my
resolve to never, ever let you go. I
would pray to the Heavens that I
would pass quickly so that I could
be with you sooner in the great
beyond."*

*She loved him more than any being in
Heaven or on earth.*

*If he were a flower, she would not
merely pluck him out of the ground
where he would ultimately die.
Rather, she would dig him out
deeply from the earth until every
last root was captured. She would*

then place him in a delicate planter
atop her windowsill where at dawn
the sunlight would warm him and
at night the moonlight would
remind him that darkness is only
temporary. She would dream about
her treasure as she slept and adore
him as the first thing she saw when
she awoke.

She doesn't have to force herself to
sleep each night tossing and
turning. She mercifully just drifts
away, always hoping that she will
dream of him. Thoughts of him are
what dance in her mind before she
slumbers.

Sometimes, she dreams of him. Other
times she wakes having no
recollection of any dreams. But she
wakes to the reality that he is, in
fact, a reality.

She wonders if, at night, he, too, does
the same. Thinks of her as he drifts

*into his dreams. Maybe, in his
dreams, he is no longer afraid of
her. He may even touch her in his
subconscious.... stroke her
hair.....caress her cheek....put his
lips upon hers.....hold her hands.*

*Some believe love means sometimes
      letting go. But a chaser never lets
      go. Why would anyone let go of
      their very own heartbeat?*

He lived in her. He lived in her heart.

*Those who do not understand a Twin
      Flame connection could never
      realize that her love of him was not
      a choice.*

It was their destiny.

8

THE TEAR COLLECTOR

"The captivating tear bottle tradition dates back nearly 3,000 years, when mourners were said to collect their tears in a tear bottle, also called a lachrymatory, and bury them with loved ones to express honor and devotion."

*Why did she make him her tear
collector?*

*She should have never seen him that
day, but she took an unexpected
detour down a road where fate
lied. He was getting out of a car.
Their eyes locked, and everything
came flooding back.*

*He didn't know why, but he was her
chosen. The stories, oh so many
countless stories. He devoured
every one. He absorbed the deepest
parts of her with every word. When
she stopped, he felt a void, an
unexplained emptiness.*

*Love. She told him that she loved him.
Those words still haunted him. He
tried to forget her under the guise
that he had someone else, but he
was captivated by her essence and
her soul, which she poured out
with each and every crafted word
and story.*

*She struck a chord in him; hit his
chiseled vanity to the core. Despite
that he claimed that he had
another, he wanted her attention
and affection all to himself. For
him to lose that made him
unsettled.*

*He ran from control, especially her
control of his heart strings.*

*For the first time he was facing the
mirror of truth, a truth he had
denied for what seemed like an
eternity.*

He was in love with her.

*He accepted with open arms his role of
tear collector. He yearned to hold
the bottle under her eyes until the
last drop of tears went into the
spout. Then, when nothing was left,
her eyes would shine brightly at
him, and he would mourn no more
for her, for she would then be his.*

*If only he were not afraid – terrified –
of feeling her soul.*

9

—————————————

TEARDROPS

"Don't go, tell me that the lights won't change,
Tell me that you'll feel the same, and we'll stay here
forever,
Don't go, tell me that the lights won't change,
Tell me that it'll stay the same."

The haunting melancholic tune Claire
De Lune popped into her head as
she walked outside. She didn't
know why this particular tune
decided to invade the airwaves of
her brain, but it did. However, it
was appropriate given how she

was feeling, how she had been
feeling.

She put a cigarette into her mouth and
lit it. Somehow, she felt that the
slow inhales of tar would serve to
quell the waves of sadness she felt,
but it didn't. Mindless puff after
mindless puff without
any satisfaction.

It was gray and misty outside. The soft
mist falling on her face reminded
her of her tears, the ones that sat
inside her eyelids refusing to come
out. Welling up was the easy part.
It was the release that was
impossible.

On her middle finger she wore a ring
with an Indian sun face on it. In
her haste to dress that morning,
she put the ring on backwards
where the sun was facing outward
instead of towards her. She tried in
vain to readjust her ring, but her

J.A. DIVINE

*finger had swelled up and it
wouldn't budge. On a day where
she needed to feel the sun facing
her, it projected outward to
everyone else but her.*

*Though no one had died, she felt a
death in her heart. It had been
days since she had heard from him.
Days ago, without warning,
everything stopped inexplicably.
She was too tired to question why.
Her mind and heart ached for him.*

*They were friends, always friends,
until things changed. They were
still friends but at the same time
they were more. They never
consummated their feelings, but
there were feelings present.*

*She had the spirit of a schoolgirl and
the heart of a woman. She basked
in her own free will to love him.
Now, just like her sunshine, he was
no more. It would be easy for her*

*to blame herself, but she knew she
was not the one at fault. Still, this
did not ease the pain of losing him.*

*She only just found out that Claire De
    Lune had lyrics, though the lyrics
    made the song even more morose.
    Tell me that it'll stay the same. Oh,
    how she wished that things hadn't
    changed, as the teardrops
    finally began to fall from her eyes.*

10

HOMESICK

"We are torn between nostalgia for the familiar and an urge for the foreign and strange. As often as not, we are homesick most for the places we have never known."
Author Unknown

*His greatest fear was himself, and
what would happen if he fell for
her. He felt as if he would lose his
entire identity, that which he
portrayed to the outside world, by
merely letting her even a*

centimeter inside himself. He was a
man, torn.

Her greatest fear was him not giving
her the chance to catch him when
he fell. To kiss him so deeply that
her very mortal existence would be
inhaled by his lips, and the life of
her, in utter surrender, drained out.

She would let him imprison her heart
and make her vessel an empty
shell, only for the want of the mere
touch and taste of his lips.

She wished that he had all the courage
and strength to let her love enter
into him, wholly and completely.

He was her familiar, her feeling of
home, and the memories of both all
she had ever known and what she
had never yet known, him.

He saw her as Pandora's box, a
present which seems valuable, but

*in reality is a curse. In Pandora's
box lies all the evils of the world.
Once Pandora opened the box,
everything escaped into the world
with the exception of hope, the only
thing left.*

*She wasn't afraid of boxes, for to her
boxes were full of hope and love.*

*Boxes reminded her of Christmases oh
so long ago. The excitement of
waking up knowing Santa Claus
had come. The running into the
living room only to find what
seemed like endless mountain of
shiny wrapped boxes of all sizes
under the bright and glistening
tree. The anticipation and
wonderment of it all delighted her
child eyes. She never worried
about what was inside the boxes,
only that they were all especially
for her.*

As she tore into box after box, all her

*wishes were fulfilled by the
magical contents containing joy,
excitement, newness, and utter
delight.*

*Unlike Pandora, there was no outpour
of evil from the boxes. There was
only love, the love presented by
Santa Claus.*

*She longed for those days of long ago,
days which she wished she could
have shared with him; together
diving into the pile of presents and
discovering the contents only for
them, together.*

*She was homesick for him, though he
was a present from her present and
not a gift from the past.*

*She yearned for the nostalgia of the
past incorporated with the present,
and always together with him
creating a new future, together.*

11
____

GILDED

"Sometimes....Sometimes our hearts.....crack a little"
Brodi Ashton, Author

By definition, gilded means covered
thinly with gold paint. Also, it
means wealthy and privileged.

In Japan, when a porcelain bowl or
other object is cracked, gold is
filled into the cracks to give it a
unique one-of-a kind appearance
to the object. This repair process is

*called Kintsugi. In the Kintsugi
process, flaws are emphasized
rather than hidden, and the
repaired piece is even more
beautiful than the original, giving
it a second life.*

*Kintsugi is built on the thought that
by embracing flaws and
imperfections, one can create an
even stronger, more beautiful
piece of art. It is the
understanding that the piece is
more beautiful for having been
broken.*

*Kintsugi is meant for inanimate objects
like bowls. Yet, your heart is filled
with cracks and open wounds of
your past. Yes, my dear one, your
heart is broken by that which I
don't know.*

*I don't need to know. I don't care to
know. Whatever has marred you in
the past shall remain there. I am*

*only concerned with the future you;
the one who hurts no more.*

*Your past need not haunt you any
more.*

*Let me be your Kintsugi artisan. I will
take my delicate brush, dip it in
flecks of gold, and gently fill in
each and every crack on your
shattered yet beautiful heart. With
every brush stroke your pain will
disappear and you will be left
with…redemption.*

*You, my dear one, are my very own
Kintsugi porcelain bowl. Your
cracks are filled with shining gold,
making it a delight to the eye
rather than an aberration. Though
you are cracked, you are more
beautiful than ever in my eyes as I
carefully fill your cracks with the
gold from my own heart.*

Only the wealthy and privileged could

*afford Kintsugi. I am a poor writer
with small hands, but whatever art
is in me, your heart will be my
canvas that I will fill with flecks of
gold until every surface is covered
in my love for you.*

*Once I am done filling your heart with
gold, your shimmer will outshine
the moon.*

*It is the moon, the full moon, where I
see your heart the most. Whenever
I see a full moon, I gaze upon it
and wish for me to be in your
heart, to forever be yours.*

*Don't we all deserve a second life, a
chance to be reborn?*

*Let me make your heart my work of
art, your beautifully wounded
heart.*

*I am an artist in my words and writing.
My hands are deft enough to dance*

J.A. DIVINE

*on a keyboard. My hands are also
skilled enough to dust gold on your
heart. My brush will move along to
a melody only you and I know.*

*The melody of us is
called.....Heartsong.*

12
____

INFINITY

*"Was it the infinite sadness of her eyes that drew him
or the mirror of himself that he found in the gorgeous
clarity of her mind?"*
F. Scott Fitzgerald

He was her mirror, so much so that he
deliberately averted her gaze on
the rare occasions they met. They
were never, ever alone. He would
never entertain the thought of
being alone with her, all for the
fear of losing himself in her. In all
settings, he knew how to control

*and compose himself. With her, he
could not fathom the thought of
falling so hard that the earth would
collapse beneath him, and into her
arms…. all from her gaze.*

*She was a writer, and her words spoke
to him from afar. He feared her
words as they spoke of him, yet he
was drawn into them. He, in turn,
always ran from the fire, forgetting
the fact that flames hold warmth
and comfort. Even the moth uses
light as a compass, and thus it's
drawn to the flame. He was her
compass, her beloved.*

*Yet, over and over again, his choice
was to flee.*

*She was sad without him, her Twin
Flame. Their mirror pulled each
other magnetically towards each
other and there was an
understanding of their purpose
through their relationship. They*

*were shared in their empathetic
traits of understanding and sharing
the feelings of others. They were
both empaths, intuitives, where
closeness and intimacy could
overwhelm them. Both were
caregivers, yet he denied the
opportunity for them to care for
one another.*

*She loved F. Scott Fitzgerald's writing,
almost as deep as her own. This
was her favorite quote:*

*"He looked at her and for a moment
she lived in the bright blue worlds
of his eyes, eagerly and
confidently."*

*His eyes were the opposite; a deep rich
brown, the color of the earth after
a rainstorm. She wanted to jump
onto his earth and feel the damp
earth encompass her body like a
safe blanket or be drowned into
him like quicksand.*

*He was an analytical thinker. She was
a dreamer. He was a Libra, the
element of air. She was water. Air
and water do not mix, except for
when the gusty winds blow upon
the vast ocean, creating waves and
ripples crashing upon the
shoreline.*

*He made her heart crash. He stirred
up the ripples in her soul. He was
the air which she inhaled deeply.*

*In a spiritual sense she was the
embodiment of the infinity symbol,
encompassing love, beauty and
power. In a disheveled world, the
infinity symbol represents
simplicity and balance and that we
have endless possibilities
before us.*

*Many times she struggled to write,
encountered blocks to her words,
trying desperately to get into his
head.*

*One day she surrendered with the
knowing thought that, in fact, their
frequency was one, and her
thoughts were in fact his. Just like
the infinity symbol, representing
new ending limitless love.*

*In him, she found her voice, her
infinity.*

13

THE LETTER

"An angel once found a demon broken and nearly dead. The angel held out his arm to help the demon. The demon looked at the angel and asked, 'Why would you save an evil demon like me?' The angel answered, 'Because without you there is no me.'"
— Patrick Jones, *The Tear Collector*

To My Dear One, My Love:

You are my demon.

You run and fear that somehow the
   love inside will be taken from you.
   You see me as a judge of your heart

*and your very soul, when in fact I
am your angel, ready to pick you
up and make us whole.*

*On this earth I have no right to judge
you or any other being. I have
nothing but love for you. Without
you, there would be no me.*

*We are a divine union and
combination. My hope and wish
are that in this lifetime our union
will become one.*

*I gave you my heart years ago, and
now I only have my words. I intend
my words to break whatever you
are running from. I wish you to
break at my feet. Then, I can
carefully and tenderly piece you
back together with gold and give
you the second life that you have
already given me.*

*I love you to the core of my being, my
Kintsugi, my beloved.*

*Know to the depth of your being that
without you, my words would be no
more. You fill the pages of my
heart.*

*In conclusion, I want to leave you with
one final thought:*

*""And you? When will you begin that
long journey into yourself?"*
— Rumi

*I began my journey long before I met
you. Begin yours. I will be with you
every step of the way, and beyond.
I will never abandon you.*

With all my love,

J.A. Divine